D0538638

THE PRINCESS AND THE PAINTER

JANE JOHNSON

FARRAR, STRAUS & GIROUX / NEW YORK

"Today Don Diego will finish his painting. I shall see it at last!" The Infanta Margarita bounced on her bed with delight.

Her ladies-in-waiting, Isabel and María, came to wash and dress the Princess. It took so long, and her clothes were so stiff, that she was hot and cross by the time they finished.

But as she went down the corridor to breakfast, the Infanta Margarita tried to look calm and stately, as a daughter of the King of Spain should.

In the dining room, alone with
María, she stopped being dignified.
Dumping a huge mound of sugar
on top of her spiced bread and milk,
she gobbled it all up.

Just then Nicolás and Maribárbola,
court dwarfs, came in with Isabel.
"Greedy guts!" they shouted, and
Nicolás did a handstand.

When the Infanta's governess
appeared, the naughty dwarfs
skipped away. "It is time for prayers."

In the royal chapel, the Princess prayed for the King and Queen. When they arrived, she hoped they would notice her. But her parents had the whole of Spain and its Empire to pray for.

With a sigh, the Infanta Margarita went to her geography lesson. "I wish I were with Don Diego instead. We would sit outside in the sunshine and draw flowers."

At last it was midday—time to attend a wedding feast for one of the Queen's ladies. The Princess ate slowly and delicately, wanting her parents to see how good she was. But they were too far away.

"Now I can go out and play!"
In the King's private garden, the
Princess ran and shrieked and
giggled until she was out of breath.

María brought rosewater for the Infanta. It made her think of the cool room where Don Diego was painting, and she longed to visit him.

On her way, the Infanta Margarita paused to watch a crowd shopping in the courtyard. "I wish I were allowed down there." Then she remembered the painting and hurried on.

She reached Don Diego's room just as her parents were leaving. "Oh, if only I'd come sooner."

But then the King saw her. "The picture is finished," he whispered. "It is his greatest work."

The Princess stared at the painting. She gasped. It was full of people she knew. But right in front, in the middle, the most important person of all, was herself.

Then the Infanta Margarita forgot that she was a princess and that Don Diego was a painter. She flung her arms around his neck and kissed him! "My dear child," he said softly, and he folded her in a warm, strong hug.

A Look at

LAS MENINAS

This is the picture that the Infanta Margarita looked at
all those years ago. She was five in 1656, when it was painted.
María, Isabel, Maribárbola, and Nicolás, grouped
around her, were real people whose names are known.
Don Diego is painting a large canvas that might be this very
picture. The cross on his chest was added later. Standing farther
back is the governess, and in the doorway is José Nieto, a courtier.
On the far wall, seen as if they were reflections in a mirror,
are the King and Queen of Spain. Most of the
people in the room seem to be looking out of the picture at us.
Perhaps they have suddenly noticed the arrival of the King and
Queen, who are watching their daughter, just as we are.

The story in this book may be true. Don Diego painted
several portraits of the Infanta Margarita, starting when she
was a baby and continuing as she grew. The pictures were
sent to her cousin Leopold of Austria, whom she married when
she was only fifteen years old. So the painter knew the Princess
well and must have loved her. His tenderness and skill make
her seem alive in this painting, for the Infanta Margarita's
friend was one of the greatest artists the world has seen:
Diego Velázquez.

For Nicola, and for D. P.

Copyright © 1994 by Jane Johnson
All rights reserved
Published simultaneously in Canada by HarperCollins*CanadaLtd*
Color separations by Hong Kong Scanner
Printed and bound in the United States of America by Berryville Graphics
Designed by Martha Rago and Lilian Rosenstreich
First edition, 1994

Library of Congress Cataloging-in-Publication Data
Johnson, Jane.
The princess and the painter / Jane Johnson. — 1st ed.
p.   cm.
[1. Velázquez, Diego, 1599-1660—Fiction. 2. Velázquez, Diego,
1599-1660. Maids of honor—Fiction. 3. Spain—Fiction.
4. Painting—Fiction. 5. Princesses—Fiction.] I. Title.
PZ7.J63216Pr 1994 93-39987 CIP AC

Velázquez's *Las Meninas* (10.5 x 9.2ft) reproduced
by permission of the Museo del Prado, Madrid, Spain.